DATE DUE

U.S. WARS

THE
INDIAN WARS

A MyReportLinks.com Book

Judy Alter

MyReportLinks.com Books
an imprint of
Enslow Publishers, Inc. E
Box 398, 40 Industrial Road
Berkeley Heights, NJ 07922
USA

MyReportLinks.com Books, an imprint of Enslow Publishers, Inc.

Library of Congress Cataloging-in-Publication Data

Alter, Judy, 1938–
  The Indian Wars / Judy Alter.
   p. cm. — (U.S. wars)
Includes bibliographical references and index.
Summary: Discusses the wars of expansion of white settlements into the
homelands of various Indian tribes and the destruction of great nations
of people.
  ISBN 0-7660-5099-8
  1. Indians of North America—Wars—Juvenile literature. [1. Indians of
North America—Wars.] I. Title. II. Series.
  E81 .A47 2002
  973—dc21
          2001008207

Printed in the United States of America

10 9 8 7 6 5 4 3 2 1

To Our Readers:
Through the purchase of this book, you and your library gain access to the Report Links that specifically back
up this book.
The Publisher will provide access to the Report Links that back up this book and will keep these Report Links
up to date on **www.myreportlinks.com** for three years from the book's first publication date.
We have done our best to make sure all Internet addresses in this book were active and appropriate when we
went to press. However, the author and the Publisher have no control over, and assume no liability for, the
material available on those Internet sites or on other Web sites they may link to.
The usage of the MyReportLinks.com Books Web site is subject to the terms and conditions stated on the
Usage Policy Statement on **www.myreportlinks.com**.
In the future, a password may be required to access the Report Links that back up this book. The password
is found on the bottom of page 4 of this book.
Any comments or suggestions can be sent by e-mail to comments@myreportlinks.com or to the address on
the back cover.

Photo Credits: © Corel Corporation, pp. 1, 3; Courtesy of Indigenous People.org, p. 37; Courtesy of
James Madison University, p. 17; Courtesy of Minnesota State University Emuseum, p. 35; Courtesy
of MyReportLinks.com Books, p. 4; Courtesy of PBS—*New Perspectives on the West*, pp. 27, 39;
Courtesy of The Ohio Historical Society, pp. 15, 16; Courtesy of The Smithsonian Institution, pp. 20,
24, 36; Courtesy of The South Dakota State Historical Society–State Archives, pp. 31, 42; Courtesy
of The University of Texas Libraries–The Perry-Castañeda Map Collection, p. 22; © Hammond World
Atlas Corporation, NJ, Lic. No. 12569, p. 12; Little Bighorn Battlefield National Monument, p. 41;
The Library of Congress, pp. 18, 32, 44; The National Archives and Records Administration, pp. 30,
43; The U.S. Bureau of the Census, courtesy of The University of Texas Libraries–The Perry-Castañeda
Map Collection, p. 15.

Cover Photo: © Corel Corporation

Cover Description: "Custer's Last Fight," author unknown

Contents

MyReportLinks.com Books
Great Books, Great Links, Great for Research!

MyReportLinks.com Books present the information you need to learn about your report subject. In addition, they show you where to go on the Internet for more information. The pre-evaluated Report Links that back up this book are kept up to date on **www.myreportlinks.com**. With the purchase of a MyReportLinks.com Books title, you and your library gain access to the Report Links that specifically back up that book. The Report Links save hours of research time and link to dozens—even hundreds—of Web sites, source documents, and photos related to your report topic.

Please see "To Our Readers" on the Copyright page for important information about this book, the MyReportLinks.com Books Web site, and the Report Links that back up this book.

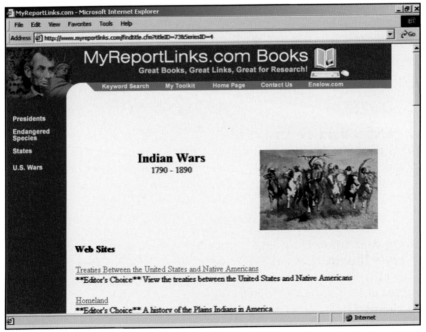

Access:

The Publisher will provide access to the Report Links that back up this book and will try to keep these Report Links up to date on our Web site for three years from the book's first publication date. Please enter **UIW2698** if asked for a password.

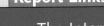

The Internet sites described below can be accessed at
http://www.myreportlinks.com

*EDITOR'S CHOICE

▶ **Treaties Between the United States and
Native Americans**
Here you will find the full text of more than twenty-five treaties
between the United States and Native Americans from the eighteenth
century to the present.

Link to this Internet site from http://www.myreportlinks.com

*EDITOR'S CHOICE

▶ **Homeland**
This PBS site offers an extended time line with links to more in-depth
information that chronicles the history of the Plains Indians in
America. Maps and images accompany the text.

Link to this Internet site from http://www.myreportlinks.com

*EDITOR'S CHOICE

▶ **Indian Removal**
This site provides information about Andrew Jackson's policy of Indian
removal, the resulting legislation, and the effects of that policy on the
Indian tribes of the South.

Link to this Internet site from http://www.myreportlinks.com

*EDITOR'S CHOICE

▶ **New Perspectives on the West**
This site, about the American West, concentrates primarily on the
nineteenth century. It includes time lines, biographies, maps, and other
resources that offer a wealth of information about the Indian Wars in
the West.

Link to this Internet site from http://www.myreportlinks.com

*EDITOR'S CHOICE

▶ **Imaging and Imagining the Ghost Dance: James
Mooney's Illustrations and Photographs, 1891–1893**
This site offers descriptions of the Ghost Dance and the Ghost Dance
movement of 1890. It features the photographs and illustrations of
James Mooney.

Link to this Internet site from http://www.myreportlinks.com

*EDITOR'S CHOICE

▶ **Black Hawk War of 1832**
Beginning with a general overview of the Black Hawk War, this site
includes a biography of Black Hawk, a chief of the Sauk and Fox tribes.
Also featured are American soldiers' accounts of the war, articles,
portraits, maps, texts of treaties, and other related documents.

Link to this Internet site from http://www.myreportlinks.com

Report Links

The Internet sites described below can be accessed at
http://www.myreportlinks.com

▶**An American Hero: Tecumseh**
This page from the James Madison University site offers a brief biography of
Tecumseh, Shawnee chief and warrior, who brought Indian tribes together in
an alliance against white settlement and the American government.

Link to this Internet site from http://www.myreportlinks.com

▶**American West: Native Americans**
More than merely a link site, the American West site offers biographies,
articles, history, and images of American Indian life and culture. This is
an excellent resource for finding other Indian War-related sites.

Link to this Internet site from http://www.myreportlinks.com

▶**The Battle of the Little Bighorn**
Here you can read an account of the Battle of the Little Bighorn as told
to Edward S. Curtis. Curtis photographed more than eighty American
Indian tribes during the last part of the nineteenth century and early part
of the twentieth.

Link to this Internet site from http://www.myreportlinks.com

▶**Black Kettle**
This page features the story of Black Kettle, a Southern Cheyenne chief who
sought peace with white settlers and the U.S. government but was betrayed by
them. Included are links to articles about Philip Sheridan, George Armstrong
Custer, William Tecumseh Sherman, and others.

Link to this Internet site from http://www.myreportlinks.com

▶**Buffalo Soldiers and Indian Wars**
This site tells the story of the Buffalo Soldiers, African Americans who fought
for the United States military in the Indian wars. Photographs, quotations,
and dozens of helpful links to related topics are included.

Link to this Internet site from http://www.myreportlinks.com

▶**The Cherokee Trail of Tears, 1838–1839**
Here you can find information about the forced removal of the Cherokee
Nation from their homeland in the American South to the Indian Territory in
Oklahoma. This march west became known as the Trail of Tears. Resources
include a time line, American Indian accounts, articles, poems, and images.

Link to this Internet site from http://www.myreportlinks.com

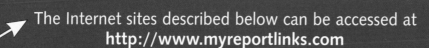
Report Links

→ The Internet sites described below can be accessed at
http://www.myreportlinks.com

Chief Joseph's Surrender
This American Memory page from the Library of Congress gives a brief
biography of Chief Joseph of the Nez Percé, who surrendered to
General Nelson Miles on October 5, 1877, after being pursued for
more than 1,000 miles.

Link to this Internet site from http://www.myreportlinks.com

Chief Sitting Bull (Tatanka Iyotake)
This site presents some quotations of the Hunkpapa Sioux chief Sitting
Bull as well as photographs and biographical information. Also
included is a remembrance of Sitting Bull by Ohiyesa (Charles A.
Eastman), a Santee Sioux.

Link to this Internet site from http://www.myreportlinks.com

Cochise and Geronimo
Here you can read the stories of the powerful Chiricahua Apache chiefs
Cochise and Geronimo. Included are excerpts from Geronimo's
autobiography, "Geronimo: His Own Story."

Link to this Internet site from http://www.myreportlinks.com

▶Crazy Horse and Custer Virtual Tour
This site contains an interactive map linking to articles about
important events of the Sioux wars and photographs of the lands where
they took place, from Fort C. F. Smith to the Little Bighorn Battlefield.

Link to this Internet site from http://www.myreportlinks.com

Crazy Horse/Tashunkewitko, Oglala
This page contains a detailed biography of Crazy Horse, the great
Lakota (Sioux) warrior, written from an American Indian perspective.

Link to this Internet site from http://www.myreportlinks.com

The Creek War
This site contains a number of articles, documents, and illustrations relating
to the Creek War. Here you will find a Creek warrior's deposition
discussing the start of the war, an 1895 history of the war, and descriptions
of the Massacre at Fort Mims and the Battle of Horseshoe Bend.

Link to this Internet site from http://www.myreportlinks.com

The Internet sites described below can be accessed at
http://www.myreportlinks.com

▶**Florida of the Seminoles**

This site contains a brief history of the Seminole as well as offering background into the Indian Wars in Florida. It includes descriptions of the battles and treaties of the Seminole Wars, biographies of those involved, photographs, and maps.

Link to this Internet site from http://www.myreportlinks.com

▶**General George Crook**

This biography of General George Crook, while discussing his Civil War and Apache War experience, focuses on his campaigns on the northern Plains. Links are provided to on-site biographies of Custer, General Nelson Miles, Red Cloud, Crazy Horse, and Sitting Bull.

Link to this Internet site from http://www.myreportlinks.com

▶**The Handbook of Texas Online—Nelson Appleton Miles**

This site offers a brief biography of General Nelson Appleton Miles, a Civil War veteran who commanded U.S. Army troops in campaigns against Indians of the southern Plains and later the Sioux and Nez Percé.

Link to this Internet site from http://www.myreportlinks.com

▶**Harmer's Defeat**

In addition to information about Little Turtle's War, this site provides biographies of Little Turtle, Blue Jacket, and General Josiah Harmar as well as profiles of the Miami, Shawnee, and Delaware tribes.

Link to this Internet site from http://www.myreportlinks.com

▶**Indian Land Cessions in the United States**

This site offers dozens of maps, treaties, and essays that show the lands ceded by American Indian groups and the lands, or reservations, they were given, or forced to move to, during the nineteenth century.

Link to this Internet site from http://www.myreportlinks.com

▶**Indian Wars**

Here you will find Indian War-related articles. Subjects include Black Hawk's War, Horseshoe Bend, scalping, and a nineteenth-century version of germ warfare.

Link to this Internet site from http://www.myreportlinks.com

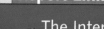 **Report Links**

The Internet sites described below can be accessed at http://www.myreportlinks.com

▶ Little Crow

On this page, you will find a biography of Sioux chief Little Crow. Facts about his youth, the factors leading to the Dakota Uprising, the events of the war, and the chief's demise are presented.

Link to this Internet site from http://www.myreportlinks.com

▶ Massacre at Wounded Knee, 1890

This site gives an overview of the events that led up to what is generally considered the last battle of the Indian Wars—the Battle, or Massacre, at Wounded Knee. It also features a map of the battle site and an eyewitness account of the events that took place.

Link to this Internet site from http://www.myreportlinks.com

▶ The Perry-Casteñeda Map Collection—Historical Maps

This comprehensive site from the University of Texas Libraries presents historical maps of the United States, including culture maps of Indian groups, maps of westward expansion and exploration, and maps of battlefields.

Link to this Internet site from http://www.myreportlinks.com

▶ Philip Henry Sheridan

Here you will find biographical information about General Philip Henry Sheridan, who served in the Civil War and was involved in campaigns during the Indian Wars.

Link to this Internet site from http://www.myreportlinks.com

▶ Red Cloud: Makhpiya-Luta (1822–1909)

On this page you will find information about Red Cloud, chief of the northern Oglala Sioux. You can also learn about his successful attacks on the Bozeman Trail as well as his involvement in the Fort Laramie Treaty, the 1887 Dawes Act, and more.

Link to this Internet site from http://www.myreportlinks.com

▶ Smithsonian American Art Museum: Native American Life and Culture

Here you will find hundreds of images of American Indian life and culture from the Smithsonian American Art Museum. Included are portraits of chiefs, depictions of battles, and illustrations of ceremonies.

Link to this Internet site from http://www.myreportlinks.com

▶ Combatants:

The United States of America

Indian tribes and nations native to the lands that make up the continental United States

▶ A Brief Time Line of Major Campaigns and Battles of the Indian Wars From 1790 to 1890

Wars in the Northwest Territory, 1790–1832

1790—Harmar's Defeat

1791—St. Clair's Defeat

1794—Battle of Fallen Timbers

1811—Battle of Tippecanoe

1832—Black Hawk's War

Wars in the South, 1813–1858

1813–1819; 1836–1837—Creek Wars

1817–1818; 1835–1842; 1855–1858—Seminole Wars

The Sioux Wars, 1854–1890

1862—Santee Uprising, Little Crow's War

1864—Sand Creek Massacre

1866—Fetterman Massacre, Red Cloud's War

1868—Massacre on the Washita

1876—Battle of Powder River

—Battle of the Rosebud

1876—Battle of Little Bighorn

1890—Battle of (Massacre at) Wounded Knee

Wars in the Northwest, 1872–1877

1877—The Pursuit of the Nez Percé

Wars in the Southwest, 1846–1886

1861–1886—The Apache wars

The Seeds of Conflict

The armed conflicts between the indigenous people of America and the Europeans and their descendants who settled in America are known collectively in American history as the Indian Wars. The Indian Wars were wars of expansion, but they were also wars that involved a clash of races and cultures. Those clashes began in the sixteenth century with fighting between Spanish explorers and Zuni warriors in what is today New Mexico. They continued through the colonial period of the seventeenth and eighteenth centuries with the English, French, and Dutch. And they lasted throughout much of the nineteenth century, more than a hundred years after the United States had become a nation.

▶ Expansion, Removal, Confinement

With the Louisiana Purchase, in 1803, the United States nearly doubled in size as it gained more than 800,000 square miles of land west of the Mississippi. The president who brought about that purchase was Thomas Jefferson. Jefferson, who had declared that "all men are created equal," saw the vast new territory as a place where American Indians could be relocated in an exchange of lands.

The United States government started moving eastern Indians west of the Mississippi during the War of 1812. By 1815 the United States began establishing western reservations. In 1830 the United States Congress, at the urging of President Andrew Jackson, passed the Indian Removal Act,

which gave the president the right to designate certain areas as lands where Indians could live. Those lands— Oklahoma, Kansas, and Nebraska—became the Indian Territory. The Indian Territory was limited, however, when Kansas and Nebraska became U.S. territories in 1854. And it ceased to be a place reserved for American Indians when Congress established the Oklahoma Territory in 1890 on unoccupied lands in the Indian Territory.

Until the middle of the nineteenth century, the presence of white settlers had, for the most part, not touched the Indian tribes living west of the Mississippi. By the 1850s, however, the United States had gained the territories of California, Oregon, New Mexico, and

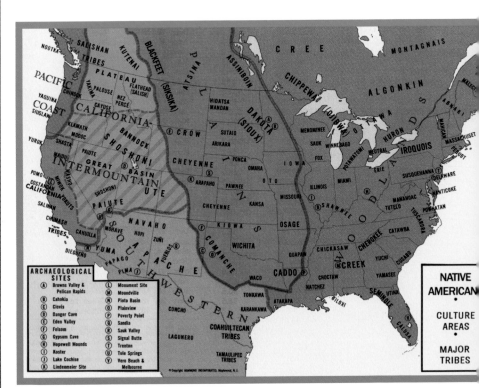

▲ This map shows where the native tribes and nations of North America lived before European settlement.

Arizona, and Texas had become a state. The discovery of gold in California in 1848 brought the forty-niners, in search of riches. Farmers and ranchers moved west to find good soil and rich grazing lands. Trails, then roads, and finally the railroad brought even more white settlers to the West, participants in the "manifest destiny" of the United States—a country that was to extend from coast to coast. The destiny of the American Indians, however, was to become "concentrated" on lands "reserved" for them by the federal government.

When the tribal customs and sacred rituals of the American Indians were threatened and their tribal lands and hunting grounds were seized, they struck back. They attacked settlers and travelers as well as the outposts the U.S. Army had established to protect them. From the 1850s until 1890, western tribes were engaged in battles with U.S. Army troops. When the fighting finally ended, in 1890, most American Indian tribes and nations were firmly concentrated on reservations. The outcome of the Indian Wars was, in almost every case, that a native people lost the lands they had called home—and their way of life was changed forever.

Chapter 2

Wars in the East

Before the American Revolution, a confederation of Indian tribes occupied the northeastern frontier of the lands held by the British in America. After the war, those tribes were pushed west to the lands surrounding the Great Lakes and the Ohio River valley, in what was known as the Northwest Territory. In the Proclamation of 1763, following the end of the French and Indian War, Great Britain forbade settlement on the lands west of the Appalachian Mountains. But by 1780, more than two thousand white families had ignored government warnings and settled in the Ohio Valley.[1] Their presence led to battles with the Indian tribes who lived there.

▶ Little Turtle's War

Some of the area's tribal chiefs favored treaties with the United States, but others resisted. In 1790, General Josiah Harmar was ordered by President George Washington to stop attacks on settlers in the Ohio country of the Northwest Territory. Harmar's army of more than three hundred regular troops and more than a thousand militia attacked and burned Miami, Shawnee, and Delaware villages near what is today Fort Wayne, Indiana.

But the Indians led by Little Turtle of the Miami tribe and Blue Jacket, a Shawnee, fought back fiercely, and many of the militia deserted the battlefield. Harmar's army lost 183 men in a crushing defeat. In 1791, Little Turtle, with the help of Tecumseh, a Shawnee chief, was again victorious in a battle against General Arthur St. Clair's

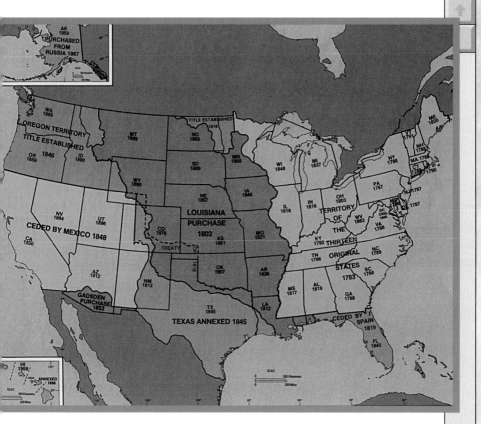

▲ The Indian Wars were wars of expansion, as the United States moved ever westward. This historical map shows when territories were acquired and when states were admitted to the Union.

soldiers along the banks of the Wabash River. In that battle, more than nine hundred U.S. soldiers and militia were killed out of twenty-one hundred, but only twenty-one Indians were killed.[2]

▶ The Battle of Fallen Timbers

But the tribes of the Northwest Territory were eventually defeated in 1794 by U.S. forces led by Revolutionary War General Anthony Wayne at a battle known as Fallen Timbers, which took place near what is today Toledo, Ohio. After their defeat at Fallen Timbers, some of the

Images - Little Turtle - Microsoft Internet Explorer

File   Edit   View   Favorites   Tools   Help   Links »

Address http://www.ohiokids.org/ohc/history/h_indian/pictures/lturtle.html

Little Turtle

Ohio's
Historic
Indians:

timelines
tribes
lifestyle
periods
events
documents
places
people
▷ images
maps
artifacts

**Northwest
Territory**
1752-1812

Little Turtle was a
great war chief of
the Miami Indians.
Under his
leadership Indian
forces defeated
two American
armies at Harmar's
Defeat and St.
Clair's Defeat.

Done   Internet

Little Turtle, a chief of the Miami Indians, won two important battles against the United States Army in the 1790s.

chiefs of the defeated Northwest tribes, including Little Turtle, decided it was best to make peace with the U.S. government. In 1795 they signed the Treaty of Greenville in which they gave up 25,000 acres of land in Ohio to the United States. One of the chiefs who did not sign was Tecumseh, who didn't want any more Indian lands to be given away in treaty.

▷ Tecumseh, Harrison, and Tippecanoe

William Henry Harrison, who had fought in the Battle of Fallen Timbers, became governor in 1800 of the Indiana Territory. Harrison talked Indian leaders into signing the 1809 Treaty of Fort Wayne in which they gave up another two-and-a-half million acres in exchange for slight payment.[3]

The Indians who were angered by their land being ceded in treaties found leaders in Tecumseh and his brother Tenskwatawa, known as the Prophet. Tenskwatawa called for all Indians in the region to settle together in towns he established, such as Prophetstown, on the Tippecanoe River in Indiana. Tecumseh, meanwhile, was busy traveling to raise an army forged by the alliance of several tribes. Urging his people and all others of the eastern Indian tribes to join him, Tecumseh demanded, "Where today are the Pequot? Where the Narraganset,

nes Madison, His Legacy: Tecumseh Biography - Microsoft Internet Explorer   _ 🗗 ✕

Edit   View   Favorites   Tools   Help   Links »   ▓

ress 🔳 http://www.jmu.edu/madison/tecumseh/tecumsehbio.htm   ▼   ℰ Go

An American Hero: Tecumseh A Brief Biography

Devin Bent (devin@bents.net)

"So live your life that the fear of death can never enter your heart. Trouble no one about their religion; respect others in their view, and demand that they respect yours. Love your life, perfect your life, beautify all things in your life. Seek to make your life long and its purpose in the service of your people. Prepare a noble death song for the day when you go over the great divide. Always give a word or a sign of salute when meeting or passing a friend, even a stranger, when in a lonely place. Show respect to all people and grovel to none. When you arise in the morning give thanks for the food and for the joy of living. If you see no reason for giving thanks, the fault lies only in yourself. Abuse no one and no thing, for abuse turns the wise ones to fools and robs the spirit of its vision. When it comes your time to die, be not like those whose hearts are filled with the fear of death, so that when their time comes they weep and pray for a little more time to live their lives over again in a different way. Sing your death song and die like a hero going home." Chief Tecumseh, Shawnee Nation, quoted in Lee Sulzman, "Shawnee History"

"Shawnee Chief Techumseh"
Chicago Natural History Museum

[Note: the fighting among the English, the colonists and the Native Americans in the Ohio Valley had gone on throughout the Revolutionary War. This article, however, begins with the end of the Revolutionary War focusing on Tecumseh and his era when he was at his height of his powers in

                                                              🌐 Internet

▲ The Shawnee chief Tecumseh forged an alliance of Indian tribes to battle U.S. troops in the Northwest Territory.

the Mohican, the Pocanoket, and many other once powerful tribes of our people? They have vanished before the avarice and oppression of the white man, as snow before a summer sun. . . ."[4]

When it became clear that Tecumseh and the Prophet were organizing a confederation to attack white settlements, Harrison camped his troops near Prophetstown and arranged to meet Tenskwatawa at council. Instead of waiting for Tecumseh to return, the Prophet's men attacked the army troops before dawn on November 7, 1811, along the Tippecanoe River. Harrison's troops stood their ground, though not without more than one hundred fifty dead and wounded, and the Shawnee withdrew. The U.S. troops claimed victory and burned Prophetstown. Tecumseh, who fought with the British in the War of 1812, was killed at the Battle of the Thames, on October 5, 1813.

▲ This painting is of the Battle of the Thames, the War of 1812 battle fought in Ontario, Canada, in which Tecumseh was killed. William Henry Harrison led the American forces that defeated the British-Indian alliance.

The Black Hawk War

After the War of 1812, white settlers began moving into the territory that is now the state of Illinois. Many members of the Sauk and Fox, two closely related tribes, were ordered west across the Mississippi River. But Black Hawk, a Sauk and Fox chief who had fought with Tecumseh during the War of 1812, refused to run. In 1829 he returned from a hunting trip to find that white families had taken over his lodge and the cornfields that provided food for his people.[5] Black Hawk had agreed to a treaty in 1804 that had given the U.S. government some 50 million acres, but he thought he was agreeing only to giving up hunting rights, not the land itself. He protested to Indian agents, men appointed by the U.S. government to handle Indian affairs, but they told him to move west across the Mississippi. He defied them by spending his summers east of the river, moving west only during the winter.

The Battle at Stillman's Run

In April 1832, Black Hawk and 2,000 men, women, and children of his tribe crossed the Mississippi and marched eastward. When he learned that Illinois volunteer militia and federal troops were ready to confront them, he sent three warriors carrying a flag of truce and five warriors to observe them to the army's camp. But when some of the volunteer militiamen saw them approaching, they fired without orders to do so, killing two of the warriors. When Black Hawk and his group of forty warriors attacked, the volunteer soldiers fled in a retreat that has become known as Stillman's Run, named for the officer in charge of the militia unit.[6]

▲ *A Sauk and Fox chief, Black Hawk resisted the government's orders that his people be moved permanently west of the Mississippi River.*

That victory spurred Black Hawk on, and he led his men on raids across the Illinois countryside. But they were eventually outnumbered, and when they tried to cross back over the river, soldiers attacked them, killing many of them. Different accounts say that Black Hawk himself either surrendered to an Indian agent[7] or was betrayed by members of the Winnebago tribe for twenty horses and a hundred dollars.[8] In any case, he was captured and imprisoned in 1832. While he was in prison, the Sauk and Fox signed a treaty in which they agreed never to return to their former land to hunt, fish, or live. They were paid $660,000 for their removal.[9]

20

Wars in the South

During the War of 1812, the Creek Indians, who lived in Georgia, Tennessee, and the Mississippi Territory, were also fighting among themselves. A band of Creek known as the White Sticks remained loyal to the United States while a group known as the Red Sticks wanted to drive all whites from their lands. In 1813, Red Sticks ambushed a small militia at Fort Mims, in what is today Alabama, killing more than four hundred settlers. The entire Creek Nation would be made to pay for that attack.

▶ Andrew Jackson vs. the Creek

After the attack on Fort Mims, the Tennessee legislature ordered General Andrew Jackson to attack the Creek. Jackson's army, which included Tennessee militiamen, White Sticks, and some Cherokee, invaded Red Stick lands, destroying many of their villages. On March 27, 1814, Jackson, with the help of 600 regular soldiers, attacked the Red Sticks at Horseshoe Bend, killing 750 of the 900 Creek. Finally, with the Treaty of Horseshoe Bend, Jackson stripped the entire Creek Nation of more than 23 million acres. Much of Alabama and Georgia were opened to white settlement, and many Creek drifted south to Florida (then owned by Spain) to join the Seminole, a closely related tribe who had separated from the Creek in the early 1700s. Other Creek were removed from their homeland and relocated in the Indian Territory.

Back   Forward   Stop   Review   Home   Explore   Favorites   History

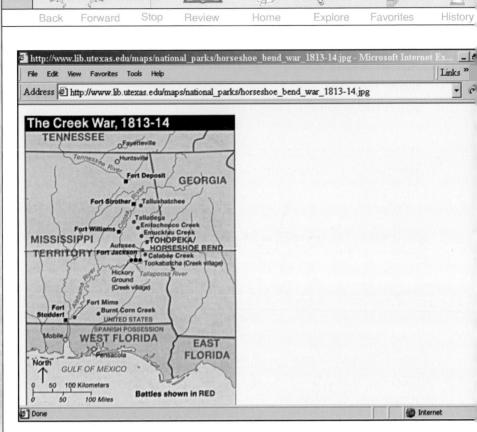

http://www.lib.utexas.edu/maps/national_parks/horseshoe_bend_war_1813-14.jpg - Microsoft Internet Ex...

File   Edit   View   Favorites   Tools   Help   Links »

Address http://www.lib.utexas.edu/maps/national_parks/horseshoe_bend_war_1813-14.jpg

The Creek War, 1813-14

TENNESSEE
Fayetteville
Tennessee River
Huntsville
Fort Deposit
GEORGIA
Fort Strother   Tallushatchee
Talladega
Enitachopco Creek
Fort Williams   Emuckfau Creek
TOHOPEKA/
MISSISSIPPI   Autosee   HORSESHOE BEND
TERRITORY Fort Jackson   Calabee Creek
Tookabatcha (Creek village)
Hickory   Tallapoosa River
Ground
(Creek village)
Fort Mims
Fort   Burnt Corn Creek
Stoddert   UNITED STATES
SPANISH POSSESSION
Mobile   WEST FLORIDA   EAST
FLORIDA
Pensacola
North
GULF OF MEXICO
0   50   100 Kilometers
0   50   100 Miles   **Battles shown in RED**

Done   Internet

▲ This map shows the locations of battles and skirmishes in Georgia, Tennessee, and the Mississippi Territory during the Creek Wars.

▶ The First Seminole War, 1817–1818

The Seminole gradually grew in number as they were joined by runaway African-American slaves who had found safety in Florida's swamps. Florida was then a Spanish territory, but the U.S. government's attention was focused on it because after the British withdrew at the end of the War of 1812, they left a fort to the Seminole and some of the fugitive slaves. In July 1816, Jackson sent Lieutenant Colonel Duncan Clinch to recover the fort and bring back the fugitive slaves, but the attack turned deadly. A gunboat skipper fired cannonballs with an extra-heavy charge into the fort, killing about three hundred

African-American men, women, and children, as well as thirty Seminole. The Seminole were so angered by that attack that they were pushed to war.

Throughout the First Seminole War, Jackson and his troops destroyed Seminole villages and supplies while the Seminole attacked settlements in Georgia. The Seminole were then persuaded to sign treaties that gave away their land and promised them food and supplies they never received. The final treaty, the Treaty of Paynes Landing, signed in 1832, forced the Seminole to leave Florida (which had become a U.S. territory) and move west of the Mississippi by 1836.

▶ The Second Seminole War, 1835–1842

But that treaty had angered Osceola, a chief whose leadership among the Seminole emerged in 1834. The government considered him such a threat that he was arrested in the spring of 1835 by General Wiley Thompson, an Indian agent. But once free, Osceola began leading attacks on white settlements. In December 1835, Osceola and eight of his warriors ambushed a wagon train that was guarded by thirty mounted militia, killing eight and wounding six. Thus began the Second Seminole War.

Osceola was now ready to wage war against the U.S. government. On December 28, he killed Wiley Thompson, the agent who had imprisoned him. That same day, more than 300 Seminole attacked a column of 110 U.S. soldiers and killed 107 of them. Only three Seminole were killed.

The Second Seminole War dragged on for seven years. Though Osceola was finally tricked into being captured and died in prison, other Seminole carried on his war. By 1838, however, the Seminole were willing to accept any part of

▲ *Osceola was finally tricked by General Thomas Jesup into attending a truce council, where he was arrested.*

Florida, no matter how small. General Thomas Jesup and other officers argued for giving the Seminole land, saying they were not in the way of white immigration. But the government ordered the fighting to continue.[1]

The war proved to be an embarrassment for Andrew Jackson. In trying to remove some fifteen hundred Seminole, the U.S. government had spent 40 million dollars and lost 1,500 soldiers.[2] Neither side can claim to have won the Second Seminole War. But most Seminole chiefs surrendered, and most of their people were moved west. There was a third Seminole War, from 1855 to 1858. Fewer than two hundred Seminole were left in Florida by its end.

Chapter 4 ►

The Southern Plains and South-western Wars

The Indians who lived on the Great Plains, which stretched from the Mississippi River to the Rocky Mountains, were a nomadic people who moved with the buffalo herds they depended on for their survival. The Plains Indians had produced great warriors who had been fighting each other for generations. Success in battle was one of the most valued parts of their culture.

In the mid-nineteenth century, as the western frontier expanded, the United States Army established forts to protect settlers and to keep travel routes such as the Oregon and Bozeman Trails open. Some of the native people whose tribal lands were being crossed by those trails fought back. Others, like Black Kettle, tried to make peace.

► Black Kettle's War

Of all the Plains tribes, the Cheyenne and Arapaho had caused the least amount of trouble to white settlers.[1] Black Kettle, a Southern Cheyenne chief, was one of the most active chiefs seeking peace and coexistence with whites.

In 1851, Black Kettle and other representatives of the Plains tribes signed the Treaty of Fort Laramie, which assigned tracts of land to individual tribes and promised them they would have those lands forever. In return, the tribes agreed to cease their attacks on settlers and travelers and to allow the U.S. government to establish military

roads and posts in western Kansas and eastern Colorado. Neither side lived up to its part of the treaty, however, as the government failed to protect the Indians, and some Indians continued attacks on wagon trains. The attacks grew after 1859, when gold was discovered in the Pikes Peak area of Colorado, bringing white prospectors, settlers, and traders into the area in great numbers.

In the fall of 1864, in an attempt to restore peace, Black Kettle met with army officers at Fort Weld near Denver. His group of Cheyenne was asked to move to a reservation on a small piece of land bounded by Sand Creek and the Arkansas River.[2] Black Kettle agreed, but the land was poor and could not sustain the Indians, since the nearest buffalo were hundreds of miles away. Many of the Cheyenne became sick on the reservation, but they believed that at least there they had the protection of the U.S. Army.

▶ The Sand Creek Massacre

That November, however, Colonel John Chivington led the Third Colorado Cavalry in a sudden and brutal attack on Black Kettle's band of Cheyenne at Sand Creek. Some two hundred Indians—including many women and children—were killed and their bodies mutilated. Black Kettle escaped, even though he went back to rescue his wife who had been badly wounded in the attack. In just a few hours, the massacre at Sand Creek had destroyed any power that the Cheyenne and Arapaho chiefs had to influence other Indians toward peace.[3] It also exemplified the frontier philosophy held by some that "the only good Indian is a dead Indian."[4]

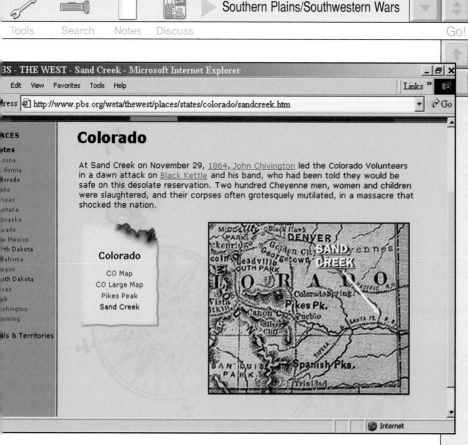

This map shows the location of Sand Creek, where more than 200 Cheyenne were massacred in November 1864.

The Massacre on the Washita

From 1865 to 1867, Black Kettle signed two more treaties that forced his people to move and gave away all rights to their lands. Even those treaties, however, failed to protect them. When militant Cheyenne and Sioux warriors pinned down an army column in the Battle of Beecher's Island in Colorado, General Philip Sheridan retaliated by ordering an attack on the Cheyenne. Sheridan gave Lieutenant Colonel George Armstrong Custer command of the Fort Dodge, Kansas, column, one of three that would meet in the valleys of the Canadian and Washita Rivers in the Indian Territory. The plan was to attack the

Cheyenne when they were most vulnerable—during the winter. The group of Cheyenne that Custer attacked, however, was Black Kettle's small band, camped on the upper Washita River. They had been nowhere near Beecher's Island and were still trying to make it to their reservation.

Even though Black Kettle's tent flew a white flag of truce, at dawn on November 17, 1868, Custer's troops attacked from four sides. Those killed included forty Indian women and children, in addition to Black Kettle and his wife. Custer, who failed to report the killing of women and children, won praise from his superior officers for the unexpected attack.[5] The massacre on the Washita River signaled the end of the Cheyenne's hope of independence. By 1869, they were confined to reservations.

▶ Wars in the Southwest—The Apache Wars

Many Indian tribes living in Arizona, New Mexico, and Texas were peaceful, but the Apache and their allies, the Navajo, were notorious fighters. They had been battling white men since the conquistadores entered their land in the sixteenth century, and they continued by conducting raids on Mexican frontier settlements in Arizona and New Mexico. The Apache wars with the U.S. Army, waged from 1861 to 1886, took more lives and cost the government more money, supplies, and horses than any other Indian war.[6]

▶ Cochise and Mangas Coloradas

Trouble between the Chiricahua band of Apache, who lived in New Mexico and Arizona, and the army began after the United States acquired those lands and tried to settle the Apache on reservations. Early in 1861, Second Lieutenant George Bascom demanded that Cochise, a

Chiricahua chief and warrior who had lived peacefully with whites for years, return a hostage that Cochise had not taken. Bascom, acting on the false accusation of a drunken rancher, arrested Cochise. But Cochise escaped, taking hostages with him and finally killing them. In retaliation, Bascom hanged three of Cochise's relatives.[7]

Mangas Coloradas, a chief of the Mimbreño band of Apache, joined Cochise in attacks on travelers passing through Apache territory as well as on the cavalry sent to protect them. But when Mangas agreed in 1863 to meet with U.S. Army officers to talk about a truce, he was captured and murdered.

By 1872 most Southwestern Indians were forced onto a reservation established at Bosque Redondo in New Mexico, but Cochise resisted until General Oliver Otis Howard, then assigned to the Southwest, agreed to establish a reservation at Apache Pass for Cochise's people. Cochise, in turn, agreed to protect travelers passing through the huge gorge. Though he kept his word, he could not control continued attacks by other Apache, and Cochise was accused of their raids.[8]

Victorio and Geronimo

In 1875 the U.S. government replaced several small reservations in the Southwest with one large one at San Carlos on the Gila River, in Arizona. Survival on the hot, dry lands of the reservation was difficult, and disease was rampant. Cochise had died in 1874, but the Apache chiefs Victorio and Geronimo continued his battles with the U.S. government. In 1877, Victorio, leader of the Ojo Caliente (Warm Springs) Apache, led three hundred of his people from San Carlos to return to their homeland in western New Mexico, but a year later they were herded

back to the reservation. Victorio and eighty of his men hid in the mountains, where they conducted a yearlong war of random raids. More warriors joined Victorio until he had about one hundred fifty men.

By the summer of 1880, Victorio and his band had been driven south into Mexico. In October 1880, Mexican soldiers surrounded Victorio during the Battle of Tres Castillos in which seventy-eight Apache were killed, and sixty-eight were captured. Victorio was killed, according to a report given by a Mexican commander, though no one knows how or when he died.[9]

But Geronimo, who had battled soldiers and settlers for more than thirty years, continued his raids. Though he willingly went to San Carlos in 1880, he fled a year later with eighty others. They returned to attack San Carlos and force several hundred Apache to join them.

General George Crook, recently assigned to the Southwest, was put in charge of returning the Apache to the reservation. He added Apache scouts to his cavalry, believing that it "took an Apache to catch an Apache."[10] They

The most persistent of the Apache fighters, Geronimo—already a legend among his people—achieved national celebrity later in life, even taking part in Theodore Roosevelt's 1905 presidential inaugural.

successfully invaded the Apache's mountain hideaway, and one by one the Apache chiefs led their people back to San Carlos. Geronimo returned in 1884 but left again a year later, taking about 125 people with him. For eighteen months, he and his men fought against 5,000 troops in a 200-by-400-square-mile area.[11]

In March 1886, after finally agreeing to surrender to General Crook, just south of the border, Geronimo changed his mind and left with a small group of Apache. Crook, criticized by his superiors for Geronimo's escape and upset with them for being asked to offer only unconditional surrender, resigned his commission. He was replaced by General Nelson Miles. It was to Miles that Geronimo finally surrendered, in August 1886.

Miles sent the Chiricahua and Warm Springs Apache to Florida, where the hot, humid conditions bred sickness among the Apache used to high, dry mountain air. Eventually the Apache were allowed to return to the West, though not to Arizona but to the Indian Territory.

General George Crook was considered by many of his fellow soldiers—and has come to be considered by historians—as one of the most skilled fighters in the Indian Wars. He was also a man who respected American Indians and thought they deserved humane treatment in defeat.

Chapter 5

The Northwestern and Northern Plains Wars

The Nez Percé, who lived west of the Rocky Mountains in what is now Idaho, Oregon, and southeastern Washington, had a history of friendship with white explorers and settlers. The Nez Percé had welcomed Lewis and Clark during their expedition in September 1805, had given them food, and had sheltered their horses while the expedition moved on by boat.[1]

Missionaries in Idaho's Lapwai Valley had taught the Nez Percé who lived there to farm and live like white men. But other Nez Percé led by Chief Joseph who lived in the Wallowa (Winding Waters) Valley, in Oregon, rejected those teachings, holding instead to the traditional ways of their people.[2]

Several Nez Percé signed a treaty in 1863 that gave up most of their land to the United States government, and they moved to the small Lapwai Reservation in Idaho. In 1855, Chief Joseph had been asked to sign a similar treaty, but he refused, saying, "I will not sign

When Chief Joseph of the Nez Percé realized he and his people could no longer escape the pursuit of the United States Army, he explained, in one of the most eloquent speeches in American history, why he and they must surrender.

your paper. . . . I have no other home than this. I will not give it up to any man. . . . Take away your paper. I will not touch it with my hand."[3] After Joseph's death, in 1871, his son, Young Joseph, became the leader of their band of Nez Percé and was also called Chief Joseph.

He continued to assert his people's independence, as his father had done, by petitioning "the Great White Father," President Ulysses S. Grant, to stay in the Wallowa Valley. In 1873, Grant withdrew the Wallowa Valley from settlement by whites, but by 1875, after gold was discovered nearby, Grant reversed his decision and opened the valley to white settlement.[4]

In 1876, General Oliver Otis Howard was sent to buy the land, which would have forced the Nez Percé onto the Lapwai Reservation, but Joseph refused to sell it. Howard gave the Nez Percé only thirty days to leave the valley, and they began the long march to Lapwai. But one night, some rebellious young warriors slipped out of the camp and killed several white men.

▶ The Pursuit of the Nez Percé

On June 17, 1877, in retaliation, U.S. cavalrymen attacked the Nez Percé camp in the Battle of White Bird Canyon, but three hundred warriors and five hundred women and children turned the troops away. Knowing they could neither return to the Wallowa Valley nor go to the Lapwai Reservation without being punished for the murder of the white men, the Nez Percé decided to flee to Canada in a thousand-mile retreat north. General Howard's men confronted them on July 11, at the Battle of Clearwater, but failed to pursue those who had scattered.

The soldiers followed close behind the Nez Percé, frequently forcing them to stop and fight. Finally, forty

miles from the Canadian border, Chief Joseph responded to a flag of truce. In one of the most eloquent speeches in American history, he spoke to his people of the need to surrender.

> I am tired of fighting. . . . It is cold and we have no blankets. The little children are freezing to death. . . . Hear me, my chiefs! I am tired. My heart is sick and sad. From where the sun now stands, I will fight no more forever.[5]

Chief Joseph surrendered to General Nelson Miles who promised him that the Nez Percé would be taken to the Lapwai Reservation. They were sent instead to Fort Leavenworth, Kansas, a swampy land that made them long for their mountain home. Chief Joseph described their surroundings at Fort Leavenworth as "a low river bottom, with no water except river water to drink and cook with."[6] Many Nez Percé died there.

By 1885, there were only 287 members of the tribe left. Though some were permitted to return to Lapwai, the government considered Chief Joseph and about 150 others too dangerous and sent them to the Colville Reservation in the state of Washington. Chief Joseph died there on September 21, 1904.

▶ Little Crow's War

The wars on the northern Plains began with Little Crow's War. Little Crow, a Santee Sioux who lived in Minnesota, had adopted many of the ways of the white man, but he had been tricked into signing two treaties that gave up most of the tribe's land. The Santee were then moved to a narrow strip of mostly barren land along the Minnesota River, where crops would not grow. Little Crow wanted to lead his people in the ways of the whites, but he was

Famous Native Minnesotans

Little Crow

le Crow was born Tayoyateduta (His Red Nation) in ca. 1810 in the Mdewakanton Dakota village of
osia. He was the first son of the chief, Wakenyantanka (Big Thunder), and his wife Minneakadawin
oman Planting in Water) and the grandson of Chetanwakuamani, who was noted in history for signing
Zebulon Pike treaty of 1805. Little Crow grew to be a very ambitious man, and one without physical
r. He acquired a reputation of being a brave warrior. During these years, he also learned to read and
te English. When his father accidentally shot and killed himself in 1846, Little Crow became the chief
is tribe. Two of his half-brothers attempted to assassinate him shortly thereafter, but only
ceeded in wounding him. Little Crow banished them, and when they returned, had them execute

▲ Little Crow, a Santee Sioux, had adopted many of the ways of the
white settlers, but he finally led his people on attacks against those
settlers after the U.S. government failed to uphold its promises in treaties.

becoming increasingly angry when supplies that had been
promised them were not delivered.

On August 18, 1862, in an unexpected attack, Little
Crow's warriors killed more than four hundred whites in
the Minnesota River valley. Two days later Little Crow led
eight hundred warriors against Fort Ridgely. The fort's
cannons saved it, and Little Crow retreated. The next day
the Sioux attacked the village of New Ulm. The citizens
were armed and ready, but the fighting was bloody. In a
week, eight hundred soldiers and settlers had been killed.[7]

The governor of Minnesota appointed militia colonel
Henry Hastings Sibley to lead an expedition against the

Santee, and Sibley's regiment defeated seven hundred Sioux and rescued many white captives. In the weeks that followed, most Santee Sioux either surrendered to Sibley or were rounded up. Sibley then organized a military court, and 303 Sioux were sentenced to hang. President Abraham Lincoln commuted the sentences of all but thirty-eight. Those thirty-eight Sioux were hanged at Mankato, Minnesota, on December 26, 1862, in the largest mass execution in American history.[8]

▶ Red Cloud's War

But the Sioux wars, begun in Minnesota, soon moved west. In 1861, a traveler named John Bozeman had found a shorter route than the Overland Trail to get to Montana's newly discovered gold fields. The trail that came to bear his name ran through the Powder River country to the mines at Virginia City, Montana Territory. The Bozeman Trail, however, crossed lands that had already been granted to the Sioux in treaty—lands on which they hunted buffalo and lands they held sacred. In 1866, several Sioux chiefs in council agreed to let white settlers cross their land. But Red Cloud, a chief of the northern Oglala Sioux, believed that whites would steal the land, no matter what treaty was signed.[9]

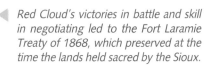

Red Cloud's victories in battle and skill in negotiating led to the Fort Laramie Treaty of 1868, which preserved at the time the lands held sacred by the Sioux.

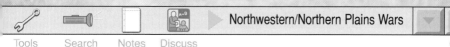

Crazy Horse/Tashunkewitko, Oglala

"A very great vision is needed and the man who has it must follow it as the eagle seeks the deepest blue of the sky. I was hostile to the white man...we preferred hunting to a life of idleness on our reservations. At times we did not get enough to eat and we were not allowed to hunt. All we wanted was peace and to be left alone. Soldiers came and destroyed our villages. Then Long Hair (Custer) came...They say we massacred him, but he would have done the same to us. Our first impulse was to escape but we were so hemmed in we had to fight."

Crazy Horse, as Remembered by Ohiyesa (Charles A. Eastman)

Crazy Horse (Tashunkewitko) was born on the Republican River about 1845. He was killed at Fort Robinson, Nebraska, in 1877, so that he lived barely thirty-three years.

▲ *Crazy Horse, an Oglala Sioux and one of their fiercest warriors, played a major role in the Sioux wars against the United States Army.*

▶ The Fetterman Massacre

From 1866 to 1868, Red Cloud's warriors attacked travelers along the Bozeman Trail, running off horses, cutting off mail delivery, and forcing wagon trains to turn back. On December 21, 1866, they attacked a woodcutting detachment from Fort Phil Kearny in north-central Wyoming. Captain William Fetterman, who demanded a chance to save the woodcutters, had bragged that he could ride through the Sioux Nation with eighty men.[10]

So he was given command of those eighty men, nearly one third of the fort's number, and sent to break up the

fighting. He was ordered, however, not to pursue the Indians, and under no circumstances was he to move beyond Lodge Trail Ridge. But Crazy Horse, one of Red Cloud's fiercest warriors, acting as a decoy, drew Fetterman and his men behind the ridge. There they were met by fifteen hundred to two thousand warriors, who massacred the entire troop.[11]

A peace treaty signed by Red Cloud at Fort Laramie in 1868 led to the Bozeman Trail being abandoned along with the forts that had protected it. The Powder River country was declared "unceded Indian territory," and all of present-day South Dakota west of the Missouri River was set aside as the Great Sioux Reservation.[12]

▶ Wars in the Black Hills

Within a year after its signing, however, the Fort Laramie Treaty of 1868 was worthless. General Philip Sheridan adopted a policy of treating all Indians on unceded land as hostile.[13] The Indians also broke the treaty, raiding settlements in Montana, Wyoming, and Nebraska.

The young warrior Crazy Horse and the Sioux chief and medicine man Sitting Bull continued resisting white settlement. They tried to stop an 1874 expedition in which George Armstrong Custer escorted surveyors for the Northern Pacific Railroad in the Black Hills, a place sacred to the Sioux. Sitting Bull's warriors had two skirmishes with Custer's troops, but they failed to stop the survey. By 1875, thousands of miners poured into the area. When attempts to persuade the Sioux to sell the land were unsuccessful, the government ordered them on December 6, 1875, to report to an agency by January 31, 1876, or be considered hostile and then hunted.

Tools   Search   Notes   Discuss   Go!

▶ The Battle of Powder River

When Sitting Bull and the other tribal leaders did not appear at the agency, General Philip Sheridan authorized General George Crook, General Alfred Terry, and Colonel John Gibbon to lead expeditions that would force the Sioux onto the reservation. Crook led 900 men in a march against the Oglala Sioux and Cheyenne in the Powder River valley but was forced to retreat. The Battle of Powder River showed the Indians, however, that the government was serious about moving them onto reservations. For protection, they gathered into one large band, under Sitting Bull's leadership. Sitting Bull and

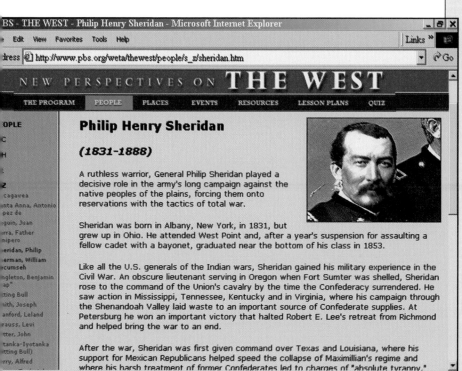

BS - THE WEST - Philip Henry Sheridan - Microsoft Internet Explorer

Edit View Favorites Tools Help   Links »

dress http://www.pbs.org/weta/thewest/people/s_z/sheridan.htm   Go

NEW PERSPECTIVES ON **THE WEST**

THE PROGRAM   PEOPLE   PLACES   EVENTS   RESOURCES   LESSON PLANS   QUIZ

Philip Henry Sheridan

(1831-1888)

A ruthless warrior, General Philip Sheridan played a decisive role in the army's long campaign against the native peoples of the plains, forcing them onto reservations with the tactics of total war.

Sheridan was born in Albany, New York, in 1831, but grew up in Ohio. He attended West Point and, after a year's suspension for assaulting a fellow cadet with a bayonet, graduated near the bottom of his class in 1853.

Like all the U.S. generals of the Indian wars, Sheridan gained his military experience in the Civil War. An obscure lieutenant serving in Oregon when Fort Sumter was shelled, Sheridan rose to the command of the Union's cavalry by the time the Confederacy surrendered. He saw action in Mississippi, Tennessee, Kentucky and in Virginia, where his campaign through the Shenandoah Valley laid waste to an important source of Confederate supplies. At Petersburg he won an important victory that halted Robert E. Lee's retreat from Richmond and helped bring the war to an end.

After the war, Sheridan was first given command over Texas and Louisiana, where his support for Mexican Republicans helped speed the collapse of Maximillian's regime and where his harsh treatment of former Confederates led to charges of "absolute tyranny."

Internet

▲ General Philip Sheridan's campaigns against the tribes of the northern and southern Plains eventually forced them onto reservations.

Crazy Horse led thousands of Indians—450 lodges, or families—on a march west into the Yellowstone country, in southeastern Montana.

The Battle of the Rosebud

They camped on Rosebud Creek and held a sun dance, a sacred ceremony. There, Sitting Bull had a vision of a great triumph for the Sioux. On June 17, 1876, General Crook approached the camp from the south, but his column was attacked by a group of Sioux warriors. Crook's men, including Crow and Shoshone Indians, battled for six hours, but they were finally forced to withdraw and return to their supply base.

The Little Bighorn

The Sioux and Cheyenne then moved their camp to the Little Bighorn River, which they called the Greasy Grass. So many more Indians joined them that they numbered nearly seven thousand. Meanwhile, General Terry held a meeting on the steamer *Far West* to plan an attack. Lieutenant Colonel George Armstrong Custer was to follow the Rosebud and cross to the Little Bighorn from the north. Terry and Colonel Gibbon were to march up the Yellowstone and Little Bighorn Rivers and take up blocking positions at the mouth of the Little Bighorn.

On June 25, 1876, Custer led his men of the Seventh Cavalry into the divide between the Rosebud and Little Bighorn Rivers. He sent a battalion commanded by Captain Frederick Benteen south to make sure that the Sioux hadn't moved into the upper valley of the Little Bighorn. When Custer approached the Little Bighorn, he spotted about forty Sioux warriors. He then sent three companies led by Major Marcus Reno after them. But

Reno's squadron found many more than forty warriors and was soon overwhelmed. Reno met Benteen, who joined him in retreat. Custer had thus split his regiment before he could draw them back together. As Benteen and Reno retreated, Custer reached the crest of a bluff and looked down at an Indian encampment larger than he could ever have imagined. Rather than waiting for Terry, and with his regiment already divided, Custer chose to attack.

▲ Lieutenant Colonel George Armstrong Custer, called "Long Hair" by the Sioux, was one of the most controversial figures of the Indian Wars, both praised for his fearlessness and condemned for his failures.

Crazy Horse led the attack from the north, while a Hunkpapa Sioux chief named Gall attacked from the south. The Sioux and Cheyenne warriors, who outnumbered Custer's men four to one, swarmed over them. Within an hour, not one of the 210 men of the Seventh Cavalry regiment under Custer's command was alive, including Custer himself.

To the United States Army, Little Bighorn was a great defeat. To the Plains Indians, it was a resounding victory, though a short-lived one. The result of Custer's defeat at Little Bighorn was that public sentiment against Indians grew, Congress increased the size of the army in the West by 2,500 cavalrymen, and the military took control of the Sioux agencies. By the late 1870s, most Plains Indians were confined to reservations.

▶ The Death of Sitting Bull

Two events marked the end of Sioux resistance to the United States government's seizure of their lands. One was the murder of Sitting Bull. The other was the Battle of Wounded Knee, also known as the Massacre at Wounded Knee.

Some Indians at the Pine Ridge Agency in South Dakota had hidden on a high plateau known as the Stronghold to hold a Ghost Dance, a ritual the Sioux believed would banish the white man from their lands and return their dead relatives and friends to them. When General Nelson Miles learned that Sitting Bull had been invited to the Stronghold for a Ghost Dance, he feared that the great chief's presence there would incite further uprisings. Miles sent Indian agency police to arrest Sitting Bull at his cabin on the Grand River early on the morning of December 15, 1890. Sitting Bull was shot and killed in the process of the arrest, as were six of his followers, his son, and six of the agency policemen.[14]

▶ The Battle of Wounded Knee

In December 1890, Chief Big Foot of the Minneconjou Sioux, at Red Cloud's

◀ *Sitting Bull's bravery and courage in battle were legendary. His death, at the hands of Indian police working for the reservation, led to the end of Sioux resistance.*

invitation, led his people toward the Pine Ridge Agency, unaware that a warrant had been issued for his arrest.

Only twenty miles from Pine Ridge, units of the Seventh Cavalry under Major Samuel Whitside stopped the Minneconjou under orders to disarm them and escort them to a cavalry camp on Wounded Knee Creek. Once there, Big Foot and his people camped for the night, surrounded by cavalry. Colonel James Forsyth then took command, and the regiment was strengthened overnight, so that troops were stationed at all sides of the Indians' camp. Four large Hotchkiss guns were pointed at the Indians' tents.

On the morning of December 29, 1890, when soldiers attempted to take the Indians' rifles, one young warrior refused to give his up, and it fired accidentally. Both sides fired upon each other, and a fierce battle followed, with hand-to-hand fighting as well as rifle fire. The Hotchkiss guns fired fifty rounds a minute. Shells exploded and pieces of metal flew everywhere, killing many Minneconjou, Big Foot among them. At least one hundred fifty Indians were killed, including women and children, and fifty were wounded. The army had twenty-five killed and thirty-nine wounded.[15] A blizzard following the battle kept the army from burying the Sioux dead until three days later. The frozen

Chief Big Foot, of the Minneconjou Sioux. ▶

▲ This photograph shows the Sioux chiefs who, on January 18,1891, surrendered at council at White Clay Creek to General Nelson Miles, effectively ending the Indian Wars of the nineteenth century.

bodies were placed in a mass grave, and the Sioux were prevented from holding a burial ceremony.

After Wounded Knee, Sioux leaders in the agency gathered in a valley to the north to debate their choices. Though several skirmishes took place between Indians and the army, indecision among the Sioux kept them from mounting a successful war. On January 15, 1891, tribal leaders surrendered to General Nelson Miles at White Clay Creek on the Pine Ridge Reservation. The Indian Wars of the nineteenth century were over.

Chapter Notes

Chapter 2. Wars in the East

1. Paula Mitchell Marks, *In a Barren Land: American Indian Dispossession and Survival* (New York: William Morrow and Company, 1998), p. 43.

2. R. Ernest Dupuy and Trevor Dupuy, *The Encyclopedia of Military History: From 3500 B.C. to the Present* (New York: HarperTrade, 1986), p. 725.

3. Marks, pp. 45–46.

4. Robert Utley and Wilcomb E. Washburn, *The American Heritage History of the Indian Wars* (New York: American Heritage Publishing Co., Inc./Bonanza Books, 1977), p. 130.

5. Ibid., pp. 147–148.

6. Ibid., p. 148.

7. Marks, p. 65.

8. Dee Brown, *Bury My Heart at Wounded Knee* (New York: Holt, Rinehart & Winston, 1970), p. 5.

9. Alan Axelrod, *Chronicle of the Indian Wars: From Colonial Times to Wounded Knee* (New York: Prentice Hall, 1993), p. 153.

Chapter 3. Wars in the South

1. Paula Mitchell Marks, *In a Barren Land: American Indian Dispossession and Survival* (New York: William Morrow and Company, Inc., 1998), p. 86.

2. Ibid., p. 85.

Chapter 4. The Southern Plains and Southwestern Wars

1. Alan Axelrod, *Chronicle of the Indian Wars: From Colonial Times to Wounded Knee* (New York: Prentice Hall, 1993), p. 196.

2. Dee Brown, *Bury My Heart at Wounded Knee* (New York: Holt, Rinehart & Winston, 1970), p. 69.

3. Ibid., p. 92.

4. Paula Mitchell Marks, *In a Barren Land: American Indian Dispossession and Survival* (New York: William Morrow and Company, Inc., 1998), p. 184.

5. Benjamin Capps, *The Old West—The Indians* (New York: Time-Life Books, 1973), p. 191.

6. Brown, p. 194.

7. Robert Utley and Wilcomb E. Washburn, *The American Heritage History of the Indian Wars* (New York: American Heritage Publishing Co., Inc./Bonanza Books, 1977), pp. 198–201.

8. Ibid., p. 247.

9. Ibid., p. 313.

10. Benjamin Capps, *The Old West—The Great Chiefs* (New York: Time-Life Books, 1975), p. 86.

11. Marks, pp. 211–212.

5. The Northwestern and Northern Plains Wars

1. Dee Brown, *Bury My Heart at Wounded Knee* (New York: Holt, Rinehart & Winston, 1970), p. 316.

2. Robert Utley and Wilcomb E. Washburn, *The American Heritage History of the Indian Wars* (New York: American Heritage Publishing Co., Inc./Bonanza Books, 1977), pp. 293–295.

3. Paula Mitchell Marks, *In a Barren Land: American Indian Dispossession and Survival* (New York: William Morrow and Company, Inc., 1998), p. 141.

4. Brown, pp. 318–320.

5. Marks, pp. 199–200.

6. Ibid., p. 200.

7. Utley and Washburn, pp. 230–231.

8. Ibid., p. 232.

9. Benjamin Capps, *The Old West—The Indians* (New York: Time-Life Books, 1973), p. 196.

10. Utley and Washburn, p. 240.

11. Ibid., p. 241.

12. Ibid., p. 244.

13. Marks, p. 189.

14. Utley and Washburn, pp. 335–338.

15. Ibid., p. 341.

Further Reading

Brown, Dee Alexander. *Bury My Heart at Wounded Knee.* Thirtieth edition. New York: Henry Holt & Company, LLC, 2001.

Connell, Kate. *These Lands Are Ours: Tecumseh's Fight for the Northwest.* New York: Raintree Steck-Vaughn Publishers, 1992.

Dillon, Richard H. *Indian Wars, 1850–1890.* New York: Smithmark Publishers, Inc., 1995.

Fox, Mary V. *Chief Joseph of the Nez Percé Indians: Champion of Liberty.* Danbury, Conn.: Children's Press, 1992.

Goldman, Martin S. *Crazy Horse: War Chief of the Oglala Sioux.* Danbury, Conn.: Franklin Watts, Inc., 1996.

Hermann, Spring. *Geronimo: Apache Freedom Fighter.* Springfield, N.J.: Enslow Publishers, Inc., 1997.

Lodge, Sally. *The Cheyenne.* Vero Beach, Fla.: Rourke Publishing, Inc., 1990.

McCall, Barbara A. *The European Invasion.* Vero Beach, Fla.: Rourke Publishing Inc., 1994.

Reedstrom, E. Lisle. *Custer's Seventh Cavalry: From Fort Riley to the Little Big Horn.* New York: Sterling Publishing Company, Inc., 1992.

Sanford, William R. *Osceola: Seminole Warrior.* Springfield, N.J.: Enslow Publishers, Inc., 1994.

Schultz, Duane. *Over the Earth I Come: The Great Sioux Uprising of 1862.* New York: Saint Martin's Press, 1993.

Viola, Herman J. *It Is a Good Day to Die: Indian Eyewitnesses Tell the Story of the Battle of Little Big Horn.* New York: Random House, Inc., 1998.

Vonvillain, Nancy. *Black Hawk, Sac Rebel.* Broomall, Pa.: Chelsea House Publishers, 1993.

Weisman, Brent R. *Unconquered People: Florida's Seminole & Miccosukee Indians.* Gainesville: University Press of Florida, 1999.

Index